If Not You, Then Who?
The Inventor in the Pink Pajamas

ISBN 978-1-951317-06-5

Published in the United States by Weeva, Inc.

First Printing, 2019

Story by David and Emberli Pridham with special assistance by Hayley Irvin
Illustrations by Hanna Luechtefeld
Design by Rachel Bostick of Weeva, Inc.

Weeva
701 Brazos Street
Austin, TX 78735

www.weeva.com
Hello@Weeva.com

Available at bookstore.weeva.com

To Brooke, Noah and Graham –
No dream is ever too big.

INTRODUCTION

Patents are inventions, which are ideas that spring to life. There are some good ideas and some not so good ones, and only the best mature into inventions. You can think of a patent as a way to protect the ideas of an inventor, and the ability to protect inventions with a patent is of great importance. The transition from an idea to an invention to a patent is fascinating and critical to mankind's advancement.

Patents are blind to the prejudices of society. It's fascinating how patents transcend gender, race, socio-economic status, and class. Especially in the United States, which built the modern global invention capture economy. Our system of invention does not just benefit a certain class, gender, or race. Rather, it's intended to be blind to all prejudice and bias.

Someone reading this book could very well be the next Thomas Edison, Alexander Graham Bell, Hedy Lamarr, or Steve Jobs. In fact, any of our readers can (and will) come up with the next great invention and change the world. We hope you enjoy our book!

Brooke could feel it when she woke up—
today was going to be a great day.

Brooke silenced her alarm with a quick

THWACK!

of the off button and sprang out of bed
like a kangaroo out of a pouch. Time to
get ready for school!

DID YOU KNOW...

Alarm clocks have existed for thousands of years. The ancient teacher Plato was known to use a water-powered alarm to wake him up for his morning lessons.

It would take until 1787 for the first mechanical alarm clock to be invented. An American clockmaker named Levi Hutchins built the device to wake himself up for work. It was over two feet tall and went off every morning at 4:00 AM!

In 1916, American inventor Frank Wehrle was granted U.S. Patent 1,181,557 for his improved alarm clock. Unlike earlier versions, Wehrle's device let users set more than one alarm. It also had a signal that automatically shut off.

It was ocean week at school, and today was Brooke's turn to give her presentation about her favorite inventor. She had chosen the famous ocean explorer Jacques Cousteau.

"What do I want to wear today?" Brooke asked herself as she sorted through her closet. "A dress? A tutu? A cape?"

Thinking about her presentation, Brooke settled on her blue whale shirt and her favorite jeans.

DID YOU KNOW...

Blue jeans were invented in 1872 by Jacob Davis. Davis was a tailor who bought his material from Levi Strauss. When one of his customers kept buying cloth to patch his torn pants, Davis had the idea to add copper rivets to the weak spots.

Davis did not have enough money to patent his idea, so he asked Strauss for his help. Strauss agreed, and in 1873, they received U.S. Patent 139,121 for their improvements in fastening pocket-openings.

Davis and Strauss decided that denim would be the best fabric for their work pants and started making denim overalls and jeans. Jeans were first sold as work pants but became fashionable in the 1950s. They have been popular ever since!

Brooke had practiced her presentation all afternoon yesterday, but she was still nervous about speaking in front of her entire class. What if she tripped walking to the front? What if she said the wrong thing?

Brooke was so focused on her presentation that she lost track of time. She was going to be late if she didn't get moving!

DID YOU KNOW...

Leonard Marraffino invented striped toothpaste in 1955. He received U.S. Patent 2,789,731 in 1957 for his striping dispenser.

Marraffino's simple design is still widely used. The main toothpaste, which is usually white, takes up most of the tube. It is connected to the nozzle at the end of the tube by a thin pipe. The stripe in the toothpaste, which is usually red or blue, actually sits on top of the white toothpaste.

When the tube is squeezed, small holes in the pipe pull the red toothpaste into the white toothpaste. The two toothpastes are thick enough that they do not mix together, and they are pushed out of the tube through the nozzle with the stripe in the middle.

What could you invent to make your morning easier?

Brooke bounded downstairs for breakfast, and to her surprise, she was the last one there! She only had time for a quick bite of toast before she had to leave for school.

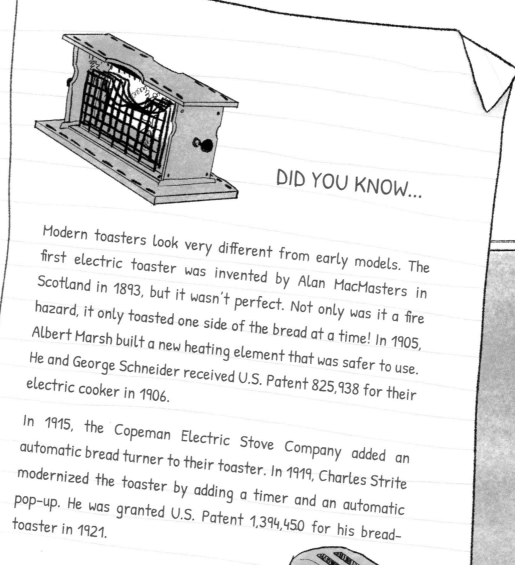

DID YOU KNOW...

Modern toasters look very different from early models. The first electric toaster was invented by Alan MacMasters in Scotland in 1893, but it wasn't perfect. Not only was it a fire hazard, it only toasted one side of the bread at a time! In 1905, Albert Marsh built a new heating element that was safer to use. He and George Schneider received U.S. Patent 825,938 for their electric cooker in 1906.

In 1915, the Copeman Electric Stove Company added an automatic bread turner to their toaster. In 1919, Charles Strite modernized the toaster by adding a timer and an automatic pop-up. He was granted U.S. Patent 1,394,450 for his bread-toaster in 1921.

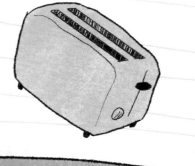

The walk to school with Grandpa was one of Brooke's favorite parts of the day. Noah always tried to run ahead, but Brooke walked with Grandpa.

Break a leg, Brooke!

Good luck today!

Not so fast, Noah!

Grandpa liked to tell her about the plants, animals, and inventions that existed in their neighborhood, and Brooke liked to listen. It seemed like Grandpa knew something about everything.

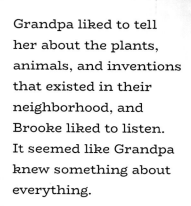

DID YOU KNOW...

William Bowerman is the father of the modern athletic shoe. Bowerman was a track coach at the University of Oregon and wanted to improve his athletes' shoes to help them run faster. To increase speed and traction, he had the idea to use a lighter rubber sole with a raised waffle design. At that time, most athletic shoes used heavy metal spikes to create traction when running. This meant that athletic shoes could only be worn on certain surfaces. Bowerman's design allowed athletic shoes to be worn on any surface and brought them into popular fashion.

In 1963, Bowerman was granted U.S. Patent 3,793,750 for his athletic shoe for artificial turf. Due to the waffle design on the sole, Bowerman called his shoe the Waffle Trainer. He actually used his wife's waffle iron to make the soles on the first pair! In 1964, Bowerman started Blue Ribbon Sports with Phil Knight, a former athlete, to make and sell Bowerman's shoe.
In 1971, they changed the name of the company to Nike, Inc.

"Grandpa, how do you become an inventor?" Brooke asked. If she was going to be an inventor like Jacques Cousteau, she needed to get started as soon as she could.

"Anyone can be an inventor," Grandpa said. "That's one of the best parts about it. All you need to get started is a good idea. Think about the guy who invented crosswalks and stop signs. He never learned to drive a car, but he still figured out how to make driving safer."

INVENTOR PROFILE: WILLIAM PHELPS ENO

William Phelps Eno was born on June 3, 1858 in New York City. Cars were not popular during his childhood, but horse-drawn carriages were causing traffic problems in big cities.

Getting stuck in a traffic jam as a child had a lasting effect on Eno. As an adult, he worked to improve traffic rules and safety. In 1903, Eno wrote the New York City traffic code. It was the first traffic code in the world. He went on to design traffic plans for London and Paris as well.

Eno is credited with many early inventions in road and traffic safety, including stop signs, crosswalks, traffic circles, and one-way streets.

"But how do you find a good idea?" Brooke asked. "Sometimes it seems like everything has already been invented."

"People invent things for all sorts of reasons," Grandpa answered. "Just look around and you'll see. Cars to help us go places faster. Seat belts to keep us safe while we're driving, and sidewalks to keep us safe while we're walking. Think of something in your life that you can make better, and then figure out how to do it."

DID YOU KNOW...

In 1923, inventor Garrett Morgan received U.S. Patent 1,475,074 for his three-position traffic signal. Morgan's signal wasn't the first. Earlier versions used two signals, one for STOP and another for GO, but policemen had to warn drivers when the signal was about to change by blowing a whistle in the intersection.

Earnest Sirrine from Chicago solved this problem when he invented the first automated traffic signal. He was granted U.S. Patent 976,939 in 1910 for his street-traffic system. To improve on Sirrine's idea, Morgan added a third light to warn drivers that the signal is about to change. Adding a third light made things safer for everyone—especially the policemen!

Before Brooke knew it, it was time to give her presentation.

"Brooke, you're up!" said her teacher, Ms. Maple.

Ms. Maple's excitement only seemed to make Brooke more nervous. She made the long walk to the front of the class, turned around to face her classmates, and began...

JACQUES COUSTEAU, OCEAN INVENTOR

BY BROOKE FAIRLEY

Jacques Cousteau was born in France in 1910. He first wanted to be a naval pilot, but an accident forced him to change his plans and pursue his love of the ocean.

Cousteau was an explorer, a scientist, a photographer, an author, a conservationist, and an inventor. His most famous inventions were for underwater diving. He invented the first underwater propulsion system, the first 35mm underwater camera, and the diving saucer.

The words glided out of Brooke's mouth exactly as she had practiced—clearly, loudly, and enthusiastically. Her presentation was going great!

The more Brooke spoke, the more her confidence grew. And it didn't hurt that she knew almost everything about Jacques Cousteau!

Cousteau's most famous invention is the Aqua-Lung. He invented it in 1943 with an engineer named Émile Gagnan. Cousteau needed a diving system that made it easier to explore, collect data, and take photos while underwater.

The Aqua-Lung was the first self-contained underwater breathing apparatus (or SCUBA) to have mainstream success. Divers liked it because it was smaller, lighter, and allowed them to stay underwater for over an hour. In 1945, Cousteau and Gagnan were granted U.S. Patent 2,485,039 for their diving unit.

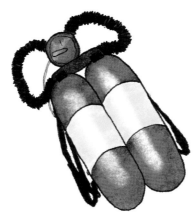

She did it! Grandpa was right. Brooke could have given this presentation underwater, upside down, and in a scuba suit. Her knowledge and practice had paid off big time.

DID YOU KNOW...

Louis de Corlieu invented modern swimfins (also known as flippers) in 1914. Early inventors like Leonardo da Vinci and Benjamin Franklin had experimented with their own fins hundreds of years before. After nearly a decade of work, de Corlieu received U.S. Patent 767,013 in 1933 for his "swimming and rescue propulsion device." In addition to the two fins on the feet, his design also had two fins shaped like spoons to wear on the hands.

Brooke raced to the car after school. She couldn't wait to tell Mom about her presentation!

How'd your presentation go, Brooke?

Swimmingly!
I think I got an A!

DID YOU KNOW...

In the 1950s, Dr. Hunter Shelden designed the first car seat belt. Dr. Shelden worked at a hospital and got the idea after seeing many patients with head injuries. It worked better than expected, and in 1966, a law was passed that required all new cars to have seat belts.

In 1959, Swedish engineer Nils Bohlin invented the modern seat belt while working at Volvo. He received U.S. Patent 3,043,625 for his three-point safety belt. In the event of a crash, it would spread energy across the passenger's chest, lap, and shoulders. Volvo knew how many lives their invention could save, so they kept the patent open and let other car makers use it for free.

Today, it was Brooke's turn to make snacks for after her soccer game. Mom had promised to help Brooke make chocolate chip cookies, her favorite.

DID YOU KNOW...

Kitchen mixers got an upgrade when electricity came into popular use in the 1880s. The first hand mixers used a handle to turn rotating parts to blend ingredients together, but when Rufus Eastman introduced the electric mixer, cooks no longer had to use the handle. Electricity turned the parts for them! He received U.S. Patent 330,829 in 1885 for his mixer.

In 1908, Herbert Johnson improved on Eastman's design by building a standing mixer. Cooks no longer had to hold the bowl or the mixer. Despite their usefulness, electric mixers didn't become popular in home kitchens until the 1920s. Now, they're a standard in many!

Mom's job was to weigh the ingredients and Brooke's job was to mix them together. Their system was working as easy as pie, and then boom—Brooke knocked a bowl of cherries right into the cookie batter! Oh no! Brooke knew they were almost certainly ruined, but Mom always looked on the bright side.

"Some of the best things were created by accident," Mom said. "Who knows? We may have just invented a new cookie."

OTHER AWESOME ACCIDENTAL INVENTIONS

1. Noah McVicker invented Play-Doh in the 1930s to clean coal stains from wallpaper. It was first known as cleaning putty.

As homes moved away from coal-powered heating, McVicker looked for other uses for his putty. He shared it with a teacher who wanted to use it for art projects. Her students loved it, so McVicker decided to sell it as a toy. In 1956, he started his own company to make and sell Play-Doh. He received U.S. Patent 3,167,440 in 1965 for his soft plastic modeling composition.

2. Popsicles first became popular in San Francisco in 1922. Back then, they were called "Epsicles" in honor of their inventor, Frank Epperson. He said he invented the frozen treat in in 1905, when he was 11 years old.

According to Epperson, he left a glass of lemonade soda with a mixing stick in it on his porch overnight. It was frozen when he went back to it the next day, much to his (and our) delight! In 1924, Epperson received U.S. Patent 1,505,592 for his frozen confectionery.

DID YOU KNOW...

Ruth Wakefield and Sue Brides invented chocolate chip cookies in 1938. Wakefield owned the Toll House Inn in Whitman, Massachusetts and wanted to serve her guests something new for dessert. Then she had the idea to chop up pieces from a chocolate bar and add them to the normal cookie batter.

The guests loved the result, and Wakefield included the recipe in her next cookbook. She called it "Toll House Chocolate Crunch Cookies." The cookies quickly became one of the country's most popular baked goods. In fact, they were so popular during World War II that soldiers wrote home to their families asking for chocolate chip cookies!

Mom was right! The cookies turned out to be delicious. Brooke couldn't wait to share her invention with her teammates.

"We'll call it the Cherry Chocolate Brookie in honor of its inventor," Mom said.

Brooke's soccer game that night was an important one. Her team, the Blue Bobcats, was playing its arch-rival, the Purple Panthers.

Brooke had missed the game-winning goal last time they played, so she and Dad had practiced almost every day since then to prepare for their rematch. Brooke was determined to win tonight.

DID YOU KNOW...

AstroTurf was invented in 1965 by James M. Faria and Robert T. Wright. It was first sold as ChemGrass. Faria and Wright improved on earlier designs by using a longer, crimped texture that made the turf more like real grass. It also cost less and was easier to take care of. They received U.S. Patent 3,332,828 for their monofilament ribbon pile product.

That same year, Judge Roy Hofheinz was building a new sports arena in Houston, Texas. It would be known as the Astrodome. To save money, Hofheinz wanted to use artificial turf in his arena instead of real grass. He decided to use ChemGrass, and it was renamed AstroTurf in honor of the new arena. In 1966, the Houston Astros played their first season at the Astrodome on AstroTurf.

DID YOU KNOW...

Soccer balls have seen many changes over the years. The earliest balls were made out of the bladders and stomachs of animals, and they would fall apart quickly. In medieval times, soccer balls were usually made by filling a leather casing with cork shavings. They wore out quickly too.

Later, leather laces (just like the laces on a football!) were also a problem. They often fell apart, and they were painful to head. In 1931, a group of inventors from Argentina developed a design without the laces.

Brooke looked towards the stands for a second, and a Purple Panther raced downfield for an easy goal. That wasn't what Brooke had practiced!

At halftime, the Blue Bobcats were losing 2-1. Drat! They would have to focus and play better if they wanted to win.

By the fourth quarter, the Bobcats had tied the game. With ten seconds left on the clock, Brooke stole the ball. It was all up to her now!

Brooke lined up her shot and kicked the ball exactly as she had practiced in the backyard with Dad. It soared over the goalie's hands and into the back of the net. The Blue Bobcats had won!

The biggest change to the soccer ball's design came when Charles Goodyear invented vulcanized rubber in 1939. Vulcanisation is the treatment of rubber to make it stronger, bouncier, and resistant to heat and cold. Soccer balls have been made with rubber cores ever since.

Rudolf and Peter R. Dehnert developed a five-sided stitching method for the outside of the ball. They received U.S. Patent 4,830,373 in 1987 for their design, giving the soccer ball its now iconic look.

Bedtime couldn't have come any quicker. Brooke was exhausted! But first, she had to brush her teeth, put on her pajamas, and find Bert the Bear. Why wasn't bedtime simpler?

DID YOU KNOW...

Teddy bears were named after former U.S. President Theodore Roosevelt, whose nickname was Teddy. The idea for the teddy bear came from an encounter he had with a bear cub in 1902.

After a cartoon of the encounter was published in a newspaper, a toymaker named Morris Michtom had the idea to make a toy based on it. Michtom and his wife made a small, cuddly bear toy and sent it to Roosevelt. They got permission to use his name and began selling it in their shop as "Teddy's bear."

The toy was an immediate success, and Michtom founded the Ideal Novelty and Toy Company. It became the largest doll-making company in the country. Even though the toy's name was eventually shortened to the "teddy bear," its popularity has only grown!

Sleep washed over Brooke with the disappearing

What's an everyday invention that you could improve?

DID YOU KNOW...

The first electric lamp was invented by British inventor Sir Humphry Davy in 1802. Davy's lamp was powered by the strongest battery in the world at that time, but it wasn't suited for everyday use. It was too bright, and as a result, it burned out quickly.

In the 1870s, British inventor Sir Joseph Swan and American inventor Thomas Edison each invented their own version of the electric lamp. Their designs were very similar, but Edison's version burned much brighter and could last for more than 1,200 hours! He received U.S. Patent 223,898 in 1880 for his electric lamp.

THINGS TO KNOW ABOUT PATENTS

WHAT IS A PATENT?

A patent is a form of **intellectual property**. The person who holds it can prevent others from making, using, or selling their invention for a set amount of time.

Intellectual property means something that was created from the mind. Inventions, books, drawings, and brand names are all forms of intellectual property.

WHAT CAN BE PATENTED?

Any device or discovery that uses a new process, machine, or material can be patented. Improvements to existing devices and discoveries can also be patented.

Laws of nature and abstract ideas cannot be patented. To be granted a patent, the applicant must include a complete description of their device or discovery.

ARE THERE DIFFERENT KINDS OF PATENTS?

Yes! **Utility patents** protect the way a device is used, made, or operated. **Design patents** protect the way a device looks.

HOW LONG DO PATENTS LAST?

Utility patents are granted for 20 years from the date the application is filed. Design patents are granted for 14 years.

WHO CAN APPLY FOR A PATENT?

Anyone! According to patent law, an inventor (or someone who is helping them) may apply for a patent for their work.

FUN FACTS ABOUT PATENTS

Australian inventor Kia Silverbrook holds more than 11,000 patents worldwide and almost 4,000 in the United States! Most of his patents are for improvements in printers and digital paper.

Thomas Edison is considered to be America's most prolific inventor. He held 1,093 patents.

The first U.S. patent was issued in 1790 to Samuel Hopkins for his process for making potash, an ingredient used in fertilizer. It was signed by George Washington!

Since 1790, over 10 million U.S. patents have been issued!

TIMELINE OF EVERYDAY INVENTIONS

1880: Thomas Edison patents his version of the electric lamp.

1893: Brothers Louis and Auguste Boutan invent the underwater camera.

1914: Louis de Corlieu first demonstrates his "swimfins" to a group of naval officers.

1923: Frank Epperson popularizes "Epsicles," now known as popsicles.

1921: Charles Strite patents his improved electric toaster.

1873: Jacob Davis and Levi Strauss patent their design for blue jeans.

1902: Morris Michtom creates the first teddy bear.

1922: Garrett Morgan invents the first three-position traffic signal.

1885: Rufus Eastman invents the first electric mixer.

1916: Frank Wehrle receives a patent for his improved alarm clock.

1959: Nils Bohlin invents the three-pointed seat belt.

1943: Jacques Cousteau and Émile Gagnan invent the Aqua-Lung, the first open-circuit scuba suit.

1965: James M. Faria and Robert T. Wright develop a new kind of artificial turf. It was later known as AstroTurf.

1955: Leonard Marraffino invents striped toothpaste.

1965: Noah McVicker patents Play-Doh.

1938: American chefs Ruth Wakefield and Sue Brides invent chocolate chip cookies.

1963: William Bowerman patents his "Waffle Trainers."

1987: Rudolf and Peter R. Dehnert patent their design for five-sided stitching on soccer balls.

STAY TUNED FOR

If not you, then who?

VOLUME 2...

FEMALE INVENTORS

HEDY LAMARR
- Inventor/actress
- Secret communication system
- Bluetooth

EDITH CLARKE
- Inventor/professor
- Graphical calculator
- First female professor of electrical engineering in the USA

ERNA SCHNEIDER HOOVER
- Inventor/mathematician
- Computerized telephone switching
- One of the first patents for computer software

MARY ANDERSON
- Inventor/real estate developer
- Windshield wipers
- Inspired by trolleys

STEPHANIE LOUISE KWOLEK
- Inventor/chemist
- Kevlar

MARTHA COSTON
- Inventor/businesswoman
- Signal flares
- Helped win the Civil War

RADIA PERLMAN
- Inventor/computer programmer
- STP protocol

BROOKE